DRAGONS

SUPER
LITTLE GIANT BOOK™ OF
DRAGONS

MICHAEL ROBERTSON &
THE DIAGRAM GROUP

Sterling Publishing Co., Inc.
New York

Library of Congress Cataloging-in-Publication Data Available

10 9 8 7 6 5 4 3 2 1

Published in 2007 by Sterling Publishing Co., Inc.
387 Park Avenue South, New York, NY 10016

Created by Diagram Visual Information Limited
195 Kentish Town Road, London, NW5 2JU, England

© 2007 Diagram Visual Information Limited

Distributed in Canada by Sterling Publishing
c/o Canadian Manda Group, 165 Dufferin Street,
Toronto, Ontario, Canada M6K 3H6

Written by   Michael Robertson and the Diagram Group
Production   Richard Hummerstone
Design   Anthony Atherton
Picture research   Neil McKenna, Patricia Robertson

Dragons have been depicted for more than 4,000 years by artists around the
world. The following illustrators provided pictures for this book: Pavel Kostal,
Kathy McDougall, Bruce Robertson, Graham Rosewarne

Sterling ISBN-13: 978-1-4027-3903-3
       ISBN-10: 1-4027-3903-6

For information about custom editions, special sales, premium and
corporate purchases, please contact Sterling Special Sales
Department at 800-805-5489 or specialsales@sterlingpub.com.

INTRODUCTION

Dragons have been around for the last 140 million years! More than a dozen human deaths were attributed to dragon bites since records began. Who did the biting? On reading this book, you will be able to answer the burning questions about dragons:

* Which dragon runs like a bicycle?

* Why are dragons so big; what is their diet; and how do they digest their food?

* What is the Order of the Dragon?

* What kind of dragon is a tail-eater?

* Which dragons were demons, and who were the heroes that killed them?

* What are the dragons in America and Asia?

* What sort of dragons lived among the Ancient Greeks and Old Slavs?

* How many types of dragons are there?

* What type of dragon could you have as a pet?

Welcome to the world
OF DRAGONS!

CONTENTS

2 DRAGON LORE

224 6 REAL DRAGONS

260 7 DRAGON TYPES

Real dragons vary as much as any other species on Earth. They come in different sizes and colors. Some have wings, others are wingless. Some are covered in scales, others by feathers. The number of toes they have can be an indication of their social status.

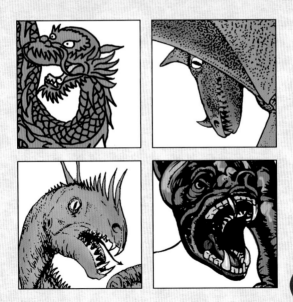

The home
of dragons

Welcome to a dragon's home

MEET YOUR DRAGONS

No dragon will happily produce its ID, even if you ask it nicely. You have to be able to identify a dragon from afar without relying on papers. You must know about their size, color, body type, skin, wings, feet, and eyes.

In case they show up in their minimalist form, you must also know about their skeletons. You must be able to tell the difference between a hen's egg and a dragon's.

You must have seen a dragon's lair already—
caves, lakes, rivers, and rocks. But have you ever
dared to enter one of them?
They can be nice and cozy
places, heated by the
flames coming from
the dragons' nostrils.
The occupants may
endear themselves to you
so much that you might want
to take them home as pets.

18

Hidden homes

Dragons live in caves. Since they don't like cold or damp conditions, they breathe fire through their nostrils, even when there are no enemies around. In that way their home becomes warm and cozy.

In 1937 a baby dragon was found hibernating in a coal mine in Newcastle, England. She currently lives in Scotland.

If a cave is warm
it often means a
dragon lives there.

SIZE

Dragons come in different sizes. Some can be as large as a whale, others as small as a squirrel.

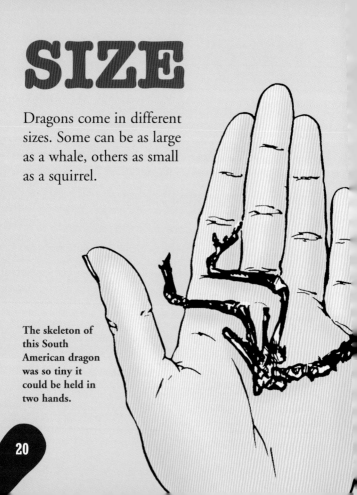

The skeleton of this South American dragon was so tiny it could be held in two hands.

The driver
of a Filipino
school bus surprised a
dragon that was twice as
long as his vehicle.

COLOR

Dragons are born different colors—usually the same color as their parents—but occasionally a rare purple or gold one is born.

Red dragons are traditionally Asian and their red and black features are used in Chinese decorations.

Green dragons represent envy and jealousy. Their sickly green flesh is used by witches in potions to inflict harm and pain.

Blue dragons are friendly and helpful, and make good pets. Yellow dragons are prized for their skin. It was used on Japanese sword handles. Ancient Greek generals had helmets made of golden dragon claws.

Gray dragons were small, about the size of bats, and were the most common. Often a castle would have more than 700 living under the rafters.

SKELETON

A dragon's skeleton supports its body, forms
levers that enable it to move, guards vital
organs, and stores blood-forming bone
marrow. Thick, solid limb bones prop up
heavy dragons, though lighter kinds
have thin-walled hollow bones.

The spine runs the length of the body,
reinforcing the neck, back, and tail, and
supporting skull and ribs—shields for the
brain, heart, and lungs. Protruding, spiked,
protective vertebrae fused to the pelvic (hip)
bones support wings and, in some species,
arm and hand bones.

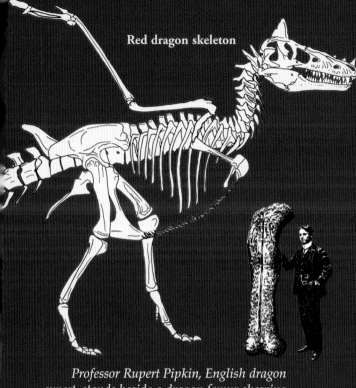

Red dragon skeleton

Professor Rupert Pipkin, English dragon expert, stands beside a dragon femur showing its colossal size. Regrettably this fossilized dragon bone was lost when the ship carrying it to America sank in a storm in 1890.

BONES

Dragon experts have found evidence of a dragon grave in a lair. The grave can be found in Tibet near Mount Everest.

When the bones found are reassembled they reveal a dragon 30 feet (9 m) long.

It is reasonable to assume that the dragon was born in the same region. When they are about to die, dragons always return to the place of their birth.

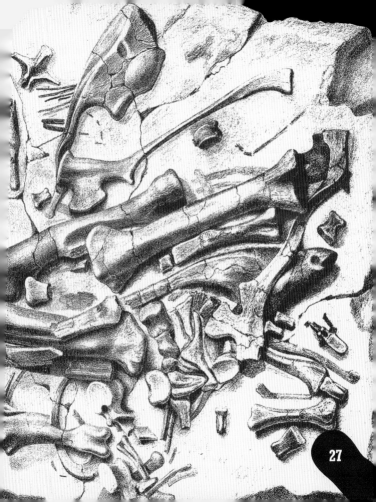

USES OF BONES

Dragons' bones are dense and heavy. They were smelted down to make weapons. King Arthur's sword and the gates of Camelot are believed to have been wrought from the melted bones of a purple dragon.

SKIN, SCALES, FEATHERS

Dragon skin is covered with protective scales.
 The purple dragon's scales are made of a brittle scallop shell material with the surface softness of pearls.
 Dragon scales overlap and slide under one another as the body turns, like the floors of baggage claim carousels in airports.

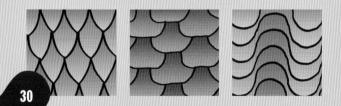

Many early dragons are said to have the head and claws of an eagle, which suggests that at least part of their bodies were covered with feathers.

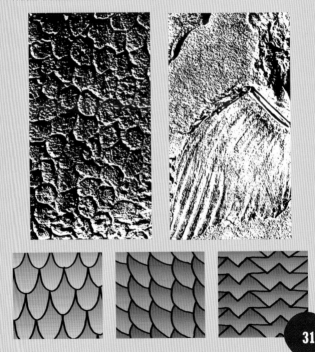

WINGS

The most fascinating feature of any dragon is its pair of wings, unless it is from a flightless species. The wings are often huge, normally larger than the dragon's body so that they can take off easily and fly fast.

Wings are just like arms and hands. Some dragons have batlike wings, where the skin is thin and stretched over a kitelike frame, whereas others have wings more like an eagle's.

Wings can be used as weapons too, but this is not recommended since the wing membranes are easily damaged.

Dragon flight

Dragons have been known to fly more than 10,000 miles (16,100 km) in search of a mate. The stronger the wings, the better they fly. Dragons with batlike wings are always seen flying within walking distance of their lair.

At lower levels they travel on thermal wind currents, not unlike eagles and other birds of prey. The main problem they have in flying is a sense of direction, as their knowledge of locations is often based on smells and familiar land features.

Dragons have a stabilizing mechanism in the front area of their brain, which enables them to stay horizontal even in heavy gusts of wind. This makes them ideal carriers of small children or nervous adults.

A dragon in full flight can move at 70 miles (112 km) per hour—as fast as an automobile on a freeway!

FEET 3

When they don't have a particular reason to fly, dragons walk short distances, usually not very far from their lair. They may visit a pond or a lake for a drink of water. That is the time when they leave their footprints in the sand or mud along riverbanks or lakesides. Their feet can have three, four, or five toes. In any case they are well equipped to feel well balanced in all situations.

4

5

The three-toed Japanese dragon

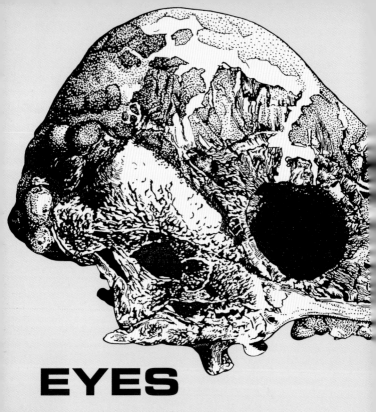

EYES

While flying, dragons can see a mouse on the ground from a mile away.

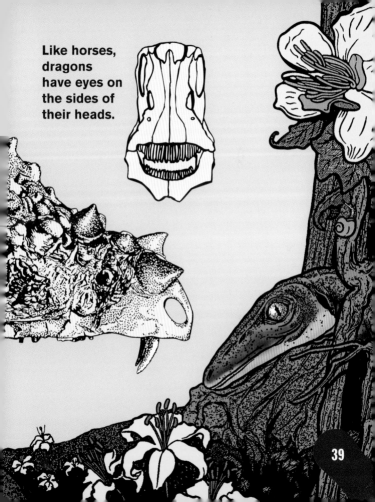

Like horses, dragons have eyes on the sides of their heads.

FOOD AND DIGESTION

Dragons are not usually threatening. The stories about knights overpowering aggressive dragons are likely to have been invented by the knights themselves. No human bones have been found in the stomachs of dead dragons or their remains. Only very rarely have dragons attacked or eaten people.

  Once a year farmers would make an "offering" of two sheep to keep dragons away from their livestock.

Eating stones

The stones (shown actual size) were necessary for the dragons' digestive systems. They would swallow them to help grind their food to pulp. The two stones shown here were found among dragon bones.

FLAMING NOSTRILS

If there is one instantly recognizable dragon feature it's their nostrils: these are usually huge and either exhaling flames or still warm during resting periods.

Dragons can make fire by using methane gas from their stomachs. They push it past two vibrating bones that spark and ignite the gas to create a "flame thrower" effect with their nostrils.

Even dragons can catch colds. But congested nostrils is the last thing dragons need. They will resort to all sorts of tricks to keep them in good working order. A huge inhaler is often the last resort.

SLOW EGGS

Dragons choose soft warm sand or lava dust in warm volcanic caves to lay their eggs. The eggs are laid in clusters.

It may take twenty years for a dragon's egg to hatch. That is, twenty dragon years, a dragon year being longer than a normal calendar year of 365 days.

Dragons lay eggs from the age of 30 through 100. They can live up to 900 years.

egg size

Dragon and hen eggs compared (actual size)

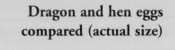

NESTS

Dragons nest in lava ash or warm earth close to recent volcanic deposits.

It is believed that the theft of a cluster of eggs from caves at the base of Mount Vesuvius in Italy caused the volcano to erupt in AD 79.

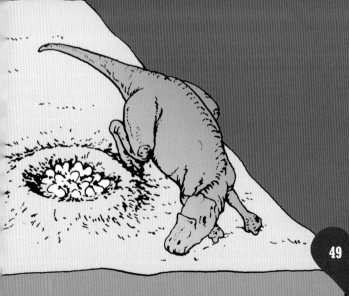

49

Dragons as pets

Many beautiful princesses were given dragons as pets. Unfortunately, if the gift was of a blue dragon, the creature would eventually grow too large to manage and the princess had to keep her pet locked in a cave or in a garden with a high wall. Pet dragons had a metal strap attached to their wings that prevented them from flying.

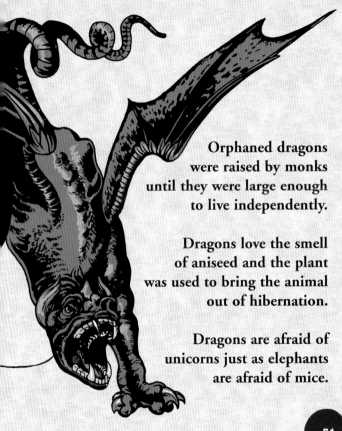

Orphaned dragons were raised by monks until they were large enough to live independently.

Dragons love the smell of aniseed and the plant was used to bring the animal out of hibernation.

Dragons are afraid of unicorns just as elephants are afraid of mice.

2 Dragon lore

Dragons are as old as humanity, if not older. The ancient Egyptians used the image of a dragon to describe the cosmos. In Europe, dragons also played a significant role in culture, both before and after the arrival of Christianity.

The Devil's dragon

In Western civilization, dragons are creatures linked to evil. The Bible refers to Satan as "The Great Red Dragon." Satan is also described as an angel that God uses to tempt Man for various reasons. In the New Testament, Satan is portrayed as an evil, rebellious demon, the enemy of God and mankind.

In John Milton's *Paradise Lost*, Satan—an ambitious underdog rebelling against Heaven—becomes the snake that tempts Adam and Eve in the Garden of Eden.

Another idea of evil force common to all cultures is witchcraft. Witchcraft is the use of certain kinds of allegedly supernatural or magical powers. A witch, like the one in the

woodcut below (1579), is a person who engages in witchcraft. This witch is holding an imp in demonic form with dragonlike wings spread and sharp claws ready to charge.

A WITCH IN THE KITCHEN

The witch in this picture is standing on a table with a sword and flame in her hand. She has called up the dragon Devil.

THE GREAT RED DRAGON

"The Great Red Dragon and the Woman Clothed in the Sun" was painted by the English poet and painter William Blake between 1806 and 1809. The painting figured in the plot of the novel *Red Dragon*, by Thomas Harris. The novel features the brilliant psychiatrist and serial killer Hannibal Lecter, a character later made famous in the film of its sequel, *The Silence of the Lambs*.

A VISION OF HELL

In Hell, thieves change into serpentlike
dragons and attack one another. In the
picture opposite, William Blake portrayed a
circle of thieves in which the condemned
attack one another as they change from men
into serpents and back again.

TORMENT &
TORTURE

Saint Anthony, a Christian martyr who lived
in the third century, was tormented by
dragons and demons. They tried to break his
faith in God by biting and pinching him, as
depicted in the illustration opposite.

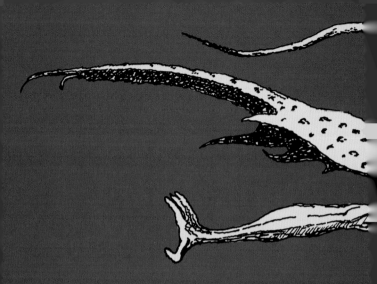

DRAGON TORMENTOR

Jacques Callot lived in early 17th century
Europe at the time of constant civil war
between Catholics and Protestants. He was a
baroque artist, draftsman, and printmaker
from France. He made etchings that
chronicled the people and the life of his
period. He would often turn to wild

landscapes and themes for inspiration. The most inspired of all his works in this line is the engraving "The Temptation of St. Anthony," where we can see a dragon of the artist's wild imagination.

THE DRAGON PRINCESS

Melusine, a woman with the lower body of a serpent or fish, appears in European folklore.

According to legend, Count Raymond de Lusignan was enchanted by Mesuline's beauty. She married him on condition that he never see her on Saturdays.

However, Raymond spied on her as she bathed one Saturday and saw her as a glistening serpent from the waist down. Realizing her secret was out, Melusine screamed, flew out the window, and was never seen again.

LEWIS CARROLL: REINVENTING MYTHOLOGY

The 19th-century English author Lewis Carroll retold past legends to a new audience. In the illustration opposite, the artist John Tenniel depicts a youthful hero battling with a reptilian dragon. Tenniel's visual inventions were ideal for Carroll's world, and their collaboration makes the stories about Alice in Wonderland timeless classics of fantasy.

Overleaf is the crazy poem by Carroll that inspired Tenniel to draw this picture.

JABBERWOCKY.

'Twas brillig, and the slithy toves
    Did gyre and gimble in the wabe;
All mimsy were the borogoves,
      And the mome raths outgrabe.

"Beware the Jabberwock, my son!
    The jaws that bite, the claws that catch!
Beware the Jubjub bird, and shun
      The frumious Bandersnatch!"

He took his vorpal sword in hand:
    Long time the manxome foe he sought—
So rested he by the Tumtum tree,
      And stood awhile in thought.

And as in uffish thought he stood,
    The Jabberwock, with eyes of flame,
Came whiffling through the tulgey wood,
      And burbled as it came!

One, two! One, two! And through and through
    The vorpal blade went snicker-snack!
He left it dead, and with its head
      He went galumphing back.

"And hast thou slain the Jabberwock?
    Come to my arms, my beamish boy!
O frabjous day! Callooh! Callay!"
      He chortled in his joy.

'Twas brillig, and the slithy toves
    Did gyre and gimble in the wabe;
All mimsy were the borogoves,
      And the mome raths outgrabe.

DREAMING OF DRAGONS

If you are not lucky enough to come across a dragon while you are awake, you might have the chance when you are asleep. You could meet the benevolent dragon of little Nemo's dreams. Little Nemo was the hero of the cartoon strip *Little Nemo in Slumberland*. The cartoon was published in the *New York Herald* from 1906. The illustrator was Winsor McCay.

Dragon blood

The first chemists to conduct experiments—
the alchemists—tried hard to find the
sorcerer's stone: a mythical substance that
could supposedly turn cheap metals into gold
and create an elixir of eternal youth.

On the page opposite you can see the *prima
materia*—a tail-biting dragon discharging the
negredo, which has to be skimmed off. This
was the first stage of the alchemical process
necessary to produce the
sorcerer's stone.

74

Draco arbor, the dragon tree.

THE DRAGON TREE

In ancient times the island of Bliss (Soqotra) had one of the busiest harbors, where merchants from Egypt, Aden, India, and Arabia came to buy medicinal plants, such as aloe, myrrh, and island cinnabar or dragon's blood, resin from the dragon tree (*Dracaena cinnabar*). Soqotra is part of the Soqotran Archipelago, and lies off the coast of Somalia in the Indian Ocean.

Draconis fructus, **the dragon fruit.**

THE ORDER OF
THE DRAGON

The Order of the Dragon is a Hungarian aristocratic order. It was founded in 1408 with a single mission: to help protect central Europe from the expanding Ottoman Empire. Members of the Order wore the image of a

dragon curled in a circle with a red cross. This was based upon the original emblem of the *Rosi-crucis*— "the cup of the waters." The original insignia is still in use today.

HERALDIC DRAGONS

Heraldry began in Europe in the Middle Ages. Knights wore armor in battle primarily to protect them from injury, but it also

Dragon passant

Dragon rampant

Wyvern

concealed their identity. Nobles therefore developed heraldry as a way of distinguishing themselves in battle.

Opinicus

Basilisk

Griffin

The *Ouroboros*—an ancient symbol showing a dragon or serpent devouring its own tail—represents cyclicality. The symbol may have originated with ancient observations and interpretations of the shape of the Milky Way.

A stone engraving of Death, set within the circle of an Ouroboros.

AROUND THE
WORLD

The image of the serpent or dragon eating its own tail is already a familiar sight in ancient Egypt (1600 BC). The pig dragons, however, of the Hongshan culture (4700–2200 BC) of China are older. From Egypt it passed to Phoenicia and then to the Greek philosophers, who gave it the name *Ouroboros*. It is also present in Hindu, Nordic, Aztec, and Native American mythology.

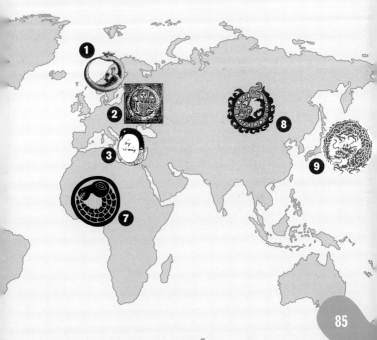

1. Scandinavian
2. European
3. Byzantine-Egyptian
4. Aztec
5. Native American
6. Navaho
7. Benin
8. Chinese
9. Japanese

Ouroboros from around the world

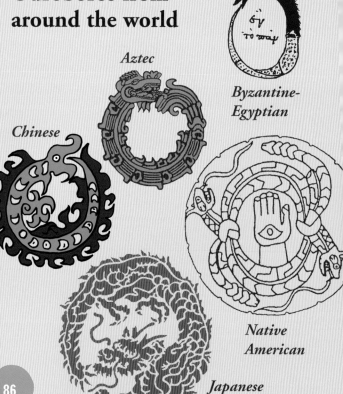

Byzantine-
Egyptian

Aztec

Chinese

Native
American

Japanese

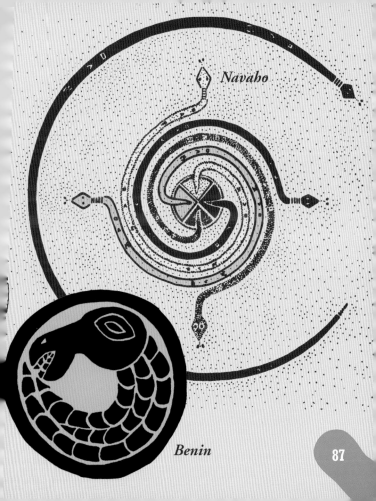

Navaho

Benin

Dragon of the cosmos

The *Ouroboros* is also known as
the *Dragon of the Cosmos*
because it represents the eternal
cosmic cycle of death and
rebirth, with its beginning and
end at the same point.

One is all, of him is everything,
for him is everything, in him
is everything. The snake is the
one; it has two symbols, good
and evil.

CHANGING MATTER

The idea of life as a cycle has a long history. Ancient peoples living far apart shared this idea and it remains present in philosophy and art today. Early alchemists believed that the *opus* (their work) proceeds in cycles, such as

that expressed by the *Ouroboros*. In these 18th-century illustrations we see the Mercurial dragon, or serpent, devour itself in fire. As a dragon it eats itself, then dies, then rises again as the sorcerer's stone.

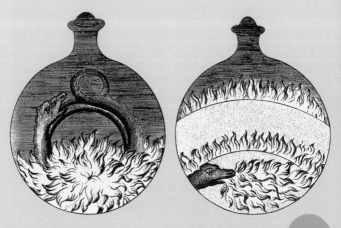

J. C. Barchusen, *Elementa chemicae*, Leiden 1718

3

Dragon slayers

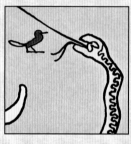

In olden times dragons were so feared that they were hunted and killed. In many parts of the world ancient beliefs suggested that dragons were guilty of making people's lives miserable. Luckily, there was always a hero on hand to slay the guilty party.

APEP, THE SERPENT OF EVIL

In Egyptian mythology, Apep was an evil demon in serpentine form, symbolizing darkness and chaos. His defeat each night, in favor of Ra, the sun god, was thought to be ensured by prayers. The Egyptians practiced a number of rituals

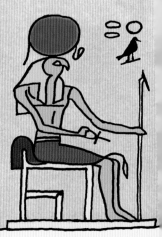

thought to ward off Apep, and assist Ra in continuing his journey across the sky. In an annual rite, called the Banishing of Apep, priests would make an effigy of Apep that was thought to contain all of the evil and darkness in Egypt, and burn it.

HERCULES, THE SLAYER OF THE
HYDRA

Hercules is a famous character in Greek mythology. He was ordered to perform twelve labors so that he could assume the throne in Mycenae. One of the labors was to slay the hydra—a dragonlike water serpent with many heads.

Hercules found the hydra and started shooting arrows at it. It attacked him, and each time he cut off one of the heads, two would grow back in its place. So Hercules had his nephew Iolaus singe the heads with fire, which prevented them from growing back. This gave Hercules time to sever the last head.

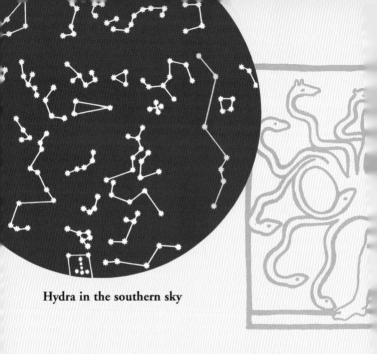

Hydra in the southern sky

Hercules and Hydra now have constellations—
groups of stars—named for them.

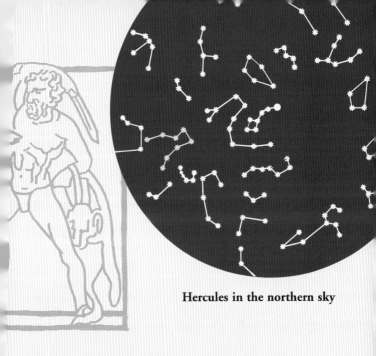

Hercules in the northern sky

On a clear night you can see Hercules in the northern sky, and Hydra in the southern sky.

CADMUS

In Greek mythology, Cadmus founded the city of Thebes.

While searching for his sister, who had been stolen by Zeus, he consulted the oracle at Delphi. He was told to follow a cow and start a settlement wherever the cow lay down.

His companions found water at a spring close to the site but were killed by the spring's guardian dragon.

Cadmus then slayed the dragon and was instructed by Athena to sow its teeth in the ground. When he did this the teeth instantly grew into warriors, who started to fight amongst themselves.

101

JASON AND THE GOLDEN FLEECE

A Greek myth tells how the hero Jason searched for the Golden Fleece—a sheepskin that would enable him to regain the throne of Thessaly.

The fleece was guarded by a hydra with seven heads and a forked tail. Jason battled it, slashing with his sword in vain.

Eventually he reached the fleece, but became entwined in the hydra's tail. With Medea's help he survived the fight, slew the hydra, and escaped with the fleece.

Medea saves Jason from the hydra.

IAΣON

SUSANOO, THE KILLER OF A DRUNKEN DRAGON

Dragons feature in Japanese Shinto mythology. Susanoo, the god of the sea and storms, encountered an elderly couple, seven of whose eight daughters had been taken by an eight-headed serpentine dragon called Orochi.

The couple promised Susanoo their eighth daughter in marriage if he slayed the serpent. So Susanoo laid out eight bowls of sake wine—one for each head—which the serpent then drank. Once it was drunk, Susanoo slayed it by cutting it into pieces.

WARRIOR VERSUS SERPENT

Egara no Heita was a 13th-century military hero in Japan, who was killed at the age of 31. This print shows an incident in which Heita slew an enormous serpent in a cave in 1207.

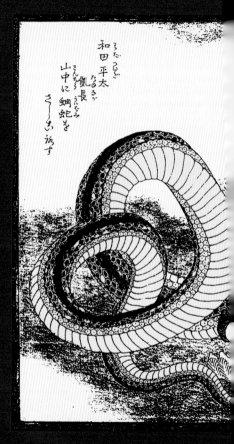

和田平太

胤長

山中に蚫蛇を

さ～ふ～ます

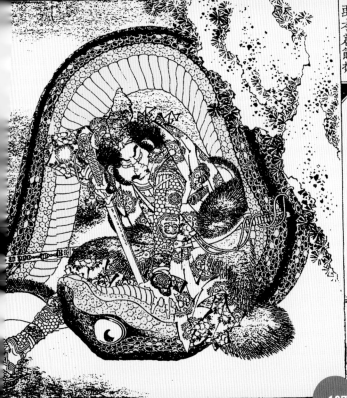

振飾葺本禹

107

THRAETAONA, THE KILLER OF THE FIRE DRAGON

Thraetaona is a hero of Persian mythology. He overthrew Azhi Dahaka—a three-headed dragon—and chained him to the mouth of a volcano.

Azhi Dahaka the three-headed dragon

SIGURD, THE DRAGON SLAYER

Sigurd is a hero of Norse mythology, who is also known as Siegfried in the German myth *Nibelungenlied*.

In both stories, the hero kills the fearsome dragon Fafnir.

Fafnir was once a man who killed his father to steal his hoard of gold—he then became a dragon to be able to guard it. Sigurd took the

gold after slaying Fafnir, but dragon gold was
always cursed, and its possession eventually
killed him.

Sigurd slays
the dragon
from below

Sigurd planned to slay Fafnir with Regin, a
swordsmith. Having killed the dragon, Sigurd
cooked its heart for Regin to eat,
inadvertently tasting its blood in the
process. The dragon's blood enabled

Sigurd tastes the dragon's blood

Sigurd to understand birdsong, from which he learned that his accomplice, Regin, intended to kill him. Sigurd therefore slew Regin first, but was later killed himself and his treasure hidden in the Rhine River.

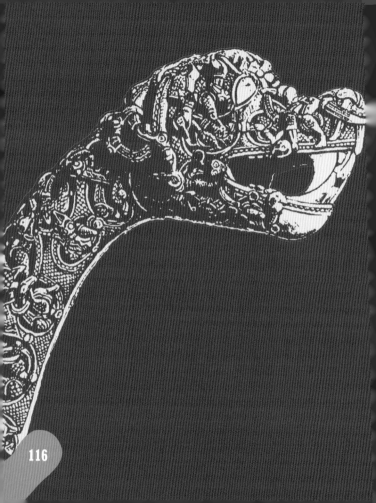

THE DEATH OF
BEOWULF

Beowulf is a famous English epic poem originating in Anglo-Saxon times (4–5th century AD). It describes Beowulf's adventures. A manuscript has survived from around AD 1000, and is now kept in the British Library in London.

  After many adventures, the last beast Beowulf encounters is a dragon. The hero kills the dragon by slashing it in half. Beowulf himself, however, also dies from the wounds he receives in the battle.

ST. GEORGE & THE DRAGON

St. George was a 4th-century Roman soldier who became a Christian martyr. The legend of him slaying a dragon appears in various versions as part of the folklore of Europe and the Near East.

The story describes how an enormous dragon made its nest at a spring that supplied a city with water. The spring was the only water supply, so the inhabitants had to confront the dragon.

To get their water they had to bribe the dragon with a daily human sacrifice. The daily victim was chosen by drawing lots.

Eventually a princess was chosen. As she was being offered to the dragon, George arrived.

He slew the dragon and saved the princess. The citizens then abandoned their pagan beliefs and converted to Christianity in gratitude.

ST. GEORGE'S DAY

The cult of St. George began in England with the return of the crusaders from the Holy Land in the twelfth century.

During the reign of Edward III (1327–77), George became accepted as the patron saint of England.

This was later immortalized in the national consciousness when the English troops in Shakespeare's play *Henry V* are rallied with the line "Cry God for Harry, England, and St. George."

123

St. George slays the dragon in
this Ethiopian depiction

St. George's cross is a red cross on a white background. It is used in countries or areas in which he is patron, such as England, Georgia, and Catalonia.

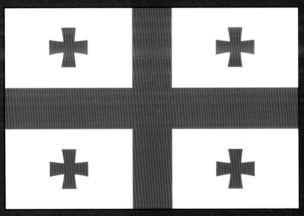

The flag of Georgia

THE LAMBTON WORM

Legend has it that on Easter Sunday, 1420, the villagers of Washington, England, were on their way to church. One young boy, the heir to Lambton Hall, was fishing by the river instead of going to church. All he caught was a small worm, which he threw into a well.

The worm grew so big over the years that it would leave the well and harass the locals. When Lambton came back from war a witch told him he must first slay the worm then kill the next creature he saw. He destroyed the worm, but unfortunately, the next living creature he saw was his father.

He couldn't bring himself to kill his father, so for the next nine generations, the Lambton family was cursed, and doomed to die abroad.

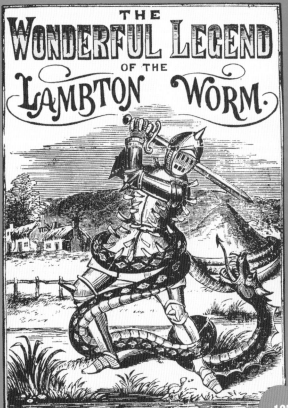

THE WONDERFUL LEGEND OF THE LAMBTON WORM

SLAVIC DRAGONS

Dragons often appear in the legends and folklore of the Slavic countries of Eastern Europe.

In Russian, a serpent is a *zmeya*, and in south Slavic languages the word is *zmaj*.

Here Dobrynia Nikitich pursues the dragon to save a princess.

Zmey Gorynych, a particular dragonlike creature of Russia and Ukraine, has three heads and two legs. It is notorious for spitting fire.

According to one legend, it was killed by Dobrynya Nikitich, a medieval Russian knight-errant. Nikitich is one of the three figures represented in Viktor Vasnetsov's painting *Bogatyrs*. The painting depicts Nikitich rescuing Zabava Putyatichna from Gorynych.

Childe Wynd thrice kisses the Laidly Worm & rescues his Sister the Princess Margaret

The Laidly Worm of Spindleston Heugh

The Laidly Worm

An English king had a beautiful daughter called Margaret and a son Childe Wynd. After his wife died he rarely went out, but one day he was out hunting when he met a beautiful woman. The king decided to make her his queen. It turned out the woman was a witch who cast a spell on Margaret. The next morning Margaret woke up as the serpentlike Laidly Worm. She crawled from her bed and crept all the way to Spindleston Heugh, a rock where she coiled herself.

People were afraid of the Laidly Worm but couldn't do anything about it—the spell could only be broken if Margaret's brother returned from his journey and kissed her three times. So the villagers sent for Childe Wynd, who came back and set his sister free with the three kisses.

The Demon with the Matted Hair

A long time ago a son was born to an Indian king. The prince's name was Bodhisattva. The priests entitled him the Prince of the Five Weapons: sword, spear, bow, battle-ax, and shield.

One day, while returning home from his studies, the prince came to a forest where the Demon with the Matted Hair lived. Halfway through the forest the serpentlike demon showed itself: it was as tall as a palm tree, had a head the size of a pagoda, eyes as big as saucers, and hair that was long and matted. The prince realized he had to fight the demon, but despite using all his weapons, he couldn't harm it. The prince, however, was clever and brave: he outwitted the demon and forced him to let him go free.

HIAWATHA'S SERPENTS

In 1855 H. W. Longfellow (1807–82), a famous American writer, published *The Song of Hiawatha.* His Hiawatha bore no relation to the 16th-century chieftain of the same name.

And Nokomis, the old woman,
Pointing with her finger westward,
Spake these words to Hiawatha:
"Yonder dwells the great Pearl-Feather,
Megissogwon, the Magician,
Manito of Wealth and Wampum,
Guarded by his fiery serpents,
Guarded by the black pitch-water.
You can see his fiery serpents,
The Kenabeek, the great serpents,
Coiling, playing in the water;
You can see the black pitch-water
Stretching far away beyond them,
To the purple clouds of sunset!"

138

ANGELS AGAINST THE APOCALYPSE

Draco is the Latin word for dragon. It means snake or serpent.

The Bible associates serpents with the Devil. This means that snakelike dragons have often symbolized evil. Before Christianity arrived in Europe, dragons were not necessarily considered evil. But since the spread of Christianity, demons opposing God, Christ, or good Christians have often been portrayed as dragons.

Throughout history many Christian saints have been depicted in the act of slaying a dragon. Angels have fought dragons too: Archangel Michael killed a dragon in a battle in Heaven.

From The New Testament, Revelation 12:3

And there appeared another wonder in heaven; and behold a great red dragon, having seven heads and ten horns, and seven crowns upon his heads.

And his tail drew the third part of the stars of heaven, and did cast them to the earth: and the dragon stood before the woman which was ready to be delivered, for to devour her child as soon as it was born.

The above 14th-century French tapestry shows
the seven-headed dragon, beast of the
Apocalypse, the Devil, and the sixth angel.

Archangel Michael

According to Christian tradition, St. Michael was set four tasks. The first was to fight Satan. He was the leader of the army of God during Lucifer's uprising, and the reason for numerous depictions of Archangel Michael thrusting a lance into a dragon's chest. In late medieval Christianity, Michael became the patron of chivalry, along with St. George. In the British honors system, a chivalric order founded in 1818 was given the name of two saints, the Order of St. Michael and St. George.

DRAGONS OF WAR

Throughout history dragons have played a role in battles and wars. Although in some cultures they have been benevolent creatures, they are more often evil and threatening, symbolizing conflict on either a human or superhuman level. The Far East has sometimes seen dragons in a positive light, not necessarily associated with war, though the picture opposite shows a dragon as the figurehead on a Chinese ship full of missiles. The dragon of Scandinavian mythology was a symbol of death and destruction. It was also the guardian of hell. Vikings of the 10th century found dragons a fitting decoration for their battle-axes.

赤龍舟圖

4

American dragons

From Central America to the mountains of Peru, early peoples drew pictures of dragons. They gave their dragons supernatural powers so that they could deal with problems the people could not solve themselves.

SERPENT
MOUND, OHIO

In ancient times, wisdom was often associated with serpents. Many ancient peoples who worshipped serpents built coiled serpentine structures. The most famous of all is the Great Serpent Mound in Adams County, Ohio. Nearly a quarter of a mile long, it was built about 500 BC.

149

FEATHERED SERPENTS

Quetzalcoatl the snake-bird was the deity of Cholulan, Mexico.

He had been expelled from the land, but pledged to return. Sentries on the east coast watched for his return. When they saw the Spanish armada approaching, their emperor, Montezuma, sent gifts to the boats, believing they heralded the arrival of Quetzalcoatl. Among the presents was a snake mask encrusted with turquoise and a feather cloak.

151

Kukulcan, plumed serpent of Mayan civilization

A wall carving in Yaschilan, Chiapas, Mexico, shows Kukulcan as the plumed serpent of the Mayas. A fascination with serpents is common throughout the ancient world of the Americas.

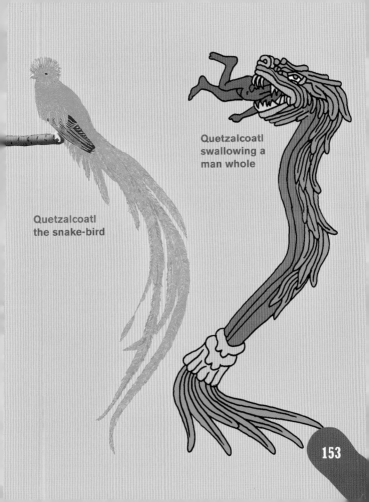

Quetzalcoatl
the snake-bird

Quetzalcoatl
swallowing a
man whole

153

The Flying-Eagle Man was a god of the Zuni, a Native American tribe, and is yet another example of civilizations endowing the

creations of human imagination with
superhuman strength, vision, and power.

This feathered serpent comes from Veracruz in Mexico. The Huaxtec people believed that by combining the qualities of serpents and birds, their god would be better able to protect them.

The Nicarao feathered serpent is a mythological symbol of a Native American tribe from Lake Managua in Nicaragua.

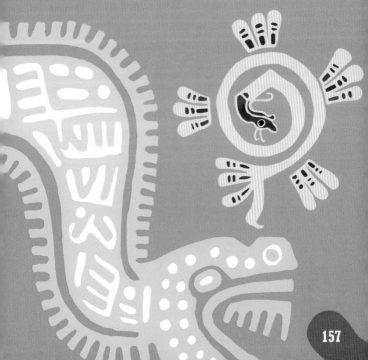

The Eagle-Man monster of the ancient
Mimbreño Indians illustrates the
preoccupation of ancient tribes with the
supernatural. The monster was probably
meant to frighten but perhaps also
to protect.

**Bird-Monster god of
the Nasa Indians**

The Nasca Indians, creators of the Bird-
Monster god, gave it the attributes they
aspired to themselves: power, wisdom, and the
ability to solve the problems humans cannot
deal with.

TWO-HEADED DRAGONS

The Incas of South America decorated their earthenware with designs such as this two-headed Chimu dragon, found on a pitcher at Truxillo, Peru.

A bowl decorated with
a chimu dragon from
South America

A two-headed chimu
dragon from the Mayan
people of Central America

161

Piasa, the Stormbird

At the end
of the 18th
century, a
painted carved
creature could be
seen in the cliffside
along the Illinois River. It
resembled a flying reptilian dragon.
The Native Americans who lived nearby
thought it was the Stormbird or
Thunderer, carved by a tribe
a long time ago.

Experts on the Mesozoic era, which covers hundreds of million of years, talk of bizarre-looking creatures such as flying saurians (pterosaurs) that lived in prehistoric times. They had combined bat- and dragonlike features. The question is, was there a real Piasa—a flying saurian—which hung by its claws on the cliffs along the Illinois River? The Illini have a legend in which Piasa is older than humankind:

When people came to live close to Piasa, the Stormbird's cave, it captured one of the tribe's warriors. The Great Chief of the Illinois, Ouatoga, pledged to put an end to Piasa. He prepared his tribe for a decisive battle in which the warriors killed Piasa with their arrows.

Pterosaurs may have hung by their hind claws from trees or cliffs.

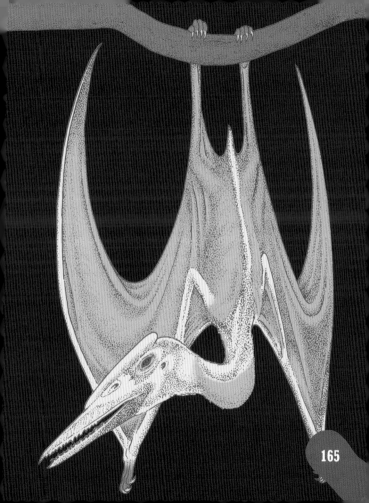

5

Asian dragons

In Asia, just like in pre-Christian Europe, dragons are loved since they are regarded as good-natured creatures, especially if well treated. And if they happen to have five claws, the Chinese royals take them as their emblem.

Asian dragons

The representation of dragons differs from culture to culture and can symbolize lots of different ideas.

In the Far East, dragons are benevolent creatures associated with prosperity and good luck. They are powerful and may make themselves visible or invisible at any time.

The Japanese share a belief in dragons with the Chinese. The dragons of Shinto tradition have sinuous serpentine bodies and are made up of elements from many other creatures in the real world. Buddhists and Taoists in China and Japan used dragons to represent obstacles that people must overcome before true happiness can be achieved.

169

India's dragons were tamed by Buddhism and adopted from an earlier tradition of the Nagas, the serpent deities. Southeast Asia also has a traditional belief in dragons.

The Vietnamese, for example, believe that their people are the descendants of a dragon. East Asian art has been strongly influenced by Buddhist concepts. Persian mythology, before the arrival of Islam, had various dragons symbolizing evil. One was a cross between a serpent and a two-legged dragon, with the head of a cockerel. Another was three-headed with six eyes and three pairs of fangs, with wings so enormous they could block out the sun. Even in Islam the abstract image of the dragon remains in art—for example in Persian carpets.

CHINESE DRAGONS

Chinese mythology is full of fascinating creatures such as Tian Gou, the heavenly dog, and Fo, the lion dog. But there are flying dragons too, symbolizing wealth and power.

There are three species of Chinese dragons: the Lung, the most powerful dragon that lives in the sky; the Li, a hornless specimen that lives in the ocean; and the Chiao, a scaly type that lives in marshes and mountain dens. The number of claws a dragon has is important. A dragon with five claws could only be used as a symbol by the Chinese Emperor.

173

INDIAN DRAGONS

The mythology of India has many examples of dragons. Many are carved in temple walls and appear in temple manuscripts. On the overleaf is Ananta, a dragon whose job it was to churn up the oceans.

Ananta, the serpent dragon, guardian of the Indian god Vishnu.

ISLAMIC DRAGONS

Although Islam does not approve of the representation of living things in art, a simplified image that is close to an abstract pattern often appears as an ornament. That is why dragons can appear on Persian carpets, though we can't exactly say where their tails, wings, or legs are.

179

Japanese dragons

Japanese mythology mirrors the environment in which the Japanese live. It doesn't surprise us that Tatsu the dragon, who represents the turbulent spirit of nature, is

constantly battling the tiger, a symbol of physical nature. These conflicts cause thunderstorms and earthquakes, which are common features of life in Japan.

KOREAN DRAGONS

Korean culture contains elements of dragon mythology. A dragon-shaped suspension loop can be seen on the top of this temple bell. The bell is used in Buddhist ceremonies. When struck, dull vibrations of the bronze bell sound throughout the temple like the waking yawn of a sleepy dragon.

183

THAI
DRAGONS

Garuda the Eagle is a lesser Hindu divinity. It appears with a golden body, an eagle's beak and wings, and the body of a man. It wears a crown like its master, Vishnu. It is huge enough to blot out the sun.

Thailand and Indonesia keep the Garuda as national symbols. The Garuda is also known in Thailand as Krut Pha, meaning Krut with stretched wings. Krut Pha is an emblem of the Thai royal family.

TIBETAN DRAGONS

Tibetan people show respect for dragons. They believe dragons live in the sky. Thunder and lightning is interpreted as the sound and sight of two of them fighting.

187

Tibetan culture has certain features in common with both China and India. Buddhism can certainly take a lot of credit for that. For example, the four dignities are mythical animals representing various aspects of the Boddhisattva attitude: strength, protection, cheerfulness. Dragons are also present in Tibetan culture, as much as in the

rest of Asia. Tibetan dragons sound like thunderclaps in the sky. These are also the sounds of compassion that can awaken us from delusion. Dragons are capable of complete communication. Displaying a dragon banner protects you from slander and enhances your reputation.

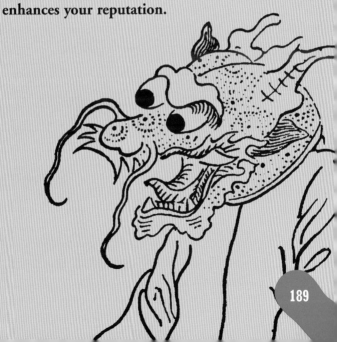

190

THE VIETNAMESE DRAGON PEOPLE

You couldn't find a tale or a legend in Vietnam without the mythical animal called Con Long, which means dragon.

This is only logical since the Vietnamese people believe they are all the descendants of a dragon. Its image is everywhere: on pagodas, dishes, clothes, furniture, and roof ridges. Dragons are believed to have supernatural powers. They are also capable of blessing people. They are, according to the Vietnamese, real guardians of the people.

NEW YEAR PARADES

Every year Chinese New Year is celebrated in big cities around the world, with Chinese communities gathering together and celebrating. One of the most fascinating features of this celebration is the New Year parade, in which dragons play a major part. The procession that slowly winds along the road is as colorful as it is noisy. The dragons are there to ward off evil spirits—it can't be done any other way.

迎龍

靜肅

迴避

清河

CHINESE IMPERIAL
DRAGONS

In ancient China the emperors had five-clawed dragons as their emblem. Each emperor was perceived as the embodiment of the dragon Yu. Yu was considered to be the mythical founder of the ancient Xia dynasty. Common people were forbidden to use the image of Yu. If they did the punishment was death. Other members of the imperial family used four-clawed dragons as their emblem. They had the right to be buried along "dragon lines," the powerful paths of dragon energy.

ASIAN DRAGON
ARTISTS

The motif of the dragon is present in art throughout Asia. Carpet weavers made designs in the shape of dragons; garments and jewelry followed the imagination of their creators into the world of dragons. Temples of various religions or their branches are marked by dragons or dedicated to one dragon. Dragons appear at the gates and roofs of building structures, mundane or sacred. Chen Rong (mid-1200s) was one of the greatest Chinese dragon painters. He imagined the dragon as the power of running water or storms. His composition style was to begin by splattering ink and water over the paper, then later alter the blotches to become dramatic representations of writhing dragons among clouds or rocks.

The first ink blots

Chen Rong began his paintings of dragons with a page of ink blots splattered on the page at random. He then filled in the spaces with his imagination and drew a dragon in a frightening pose.

Enter the dragon

The finished painting

A Japanese god with his pet dragon

A Japanese dragon of the sea

Temple dragons

The wild energy of dragons is reined in by the Asian sculptors whose imaginations seemed to know no boundaries.

DRAGON BOWLS AND VASES

A Chinese artist painted this dragon onto a plate five hundred years ago. The plate was given to a visiting ruler or his ambassador to express the emperor's pleasure at their meeting.

A three-toed
people's
dragon

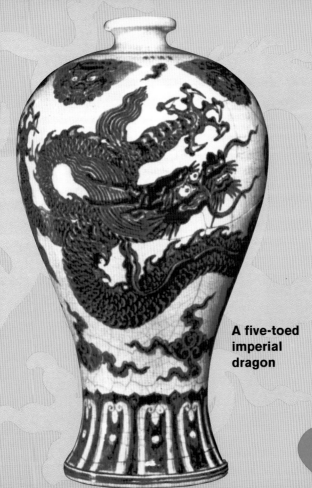

A five-toed
imperial
dragon

208

DRAGON KITES

The earliest written account of kite flying was about 200 years before the birth of Christ. A Chinese general flew a kite over the walls of a city he was attacking. He wanted to see how far his soldiers would have to tunnel to reach past the defense line.

The art of kite flying in East Asian cultures has a long and colorful tradition but today it is popular everywhere.

In recent years, multiline kite flying has developed into a sport. The competitors who fly their kites with the best skill win.

CHILDREN'S TOYS

The creators of modern computer games that involve dragons have invented nothing new. Children's imaginations have always been fired up by the image of a dragon and its creative powers and potential.

Dragons have the ability to change their shape and size and even to vanish altogether. Different types of dragons support the abodes of the gods, create wind and rain, rule over springs and rivers, and guard hidden treasures. In the picture opposite, children playing outside hold a dragon and a ball representing a flaming pearl.

DRAGON TATTOOS

Dragons have found their way into every nook and cranny on the planet. Even on people's chests, arms, and legs, dragons are popular tattoo patterns. Some of these tattoos are works of art, others are plain scary.

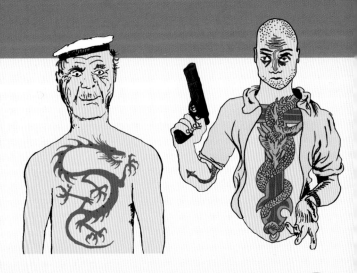

CHINESE YEARS

In Asian astrology there are twelve symbolic animals and the five elements. Although this astrological system originated in China, it is widely practiced in other Asian countries that, historically, came under Chinese influence. For example, many Japanese and Vietnamese people use Chinese astrology to interpret their lives.

Chinese astrology is governed by the influence of the Moon in a twelve-year cycle, with each year ruled by an animal: rat, ox, tiger, rabbit, dragon, snake, horse, goat, monkey, rooster, dog, or pig.

THE DRAGON PERSONALITY

The dragon is the only mythical animal in the
Chinese zodiac. Dragons have magnetic,
persuasive personalities and are capable of
great success or spectacular failure. Normally,
however, whatever they set their hearts on
doing, they do well: the secret is their great
faith in themselves. On the negative side,
dragons are renowned for not finishing what
they have begun.

The table at the top of the opposite page details the
general personality traits of those people who are
typical dragons, at both their best and worst.

Positive	Negative
• visionary	• demanding
• dynamic	• impatient
• idealistic	• intolerant
• perfectionist	• gullible
• scrupulous	• dissatisfied
• lucky	• overpowering
• successful	• irritable
• enthusiastic	• abrupt
• sentimental	• naive
• healthy	• overzealous
• voluble	• eccentric
• irresistible	• proud
• exciting	• tactless
• intelligent	• short-tempered

Lunar years ruled
by the dragon and their elements

1904	16 Feb 1904	03 Feb 1905	wood
1916	03 Feb 1916	22 Jan 1917	fire
1928	23 Jan 1928	09 Feb 1929	earth
1940	08 Feb 1940	26 Jan 1941	metal
1952	27 Jan 1952	13 Feb 1953	water
1964	13 Feb 1964	01 Feb 1965	wood
1976	31 Jan 1976	17 Feb 1977	fire
1988	17 Feb 1988	05 Feb 1989	earth
2000	05 Feb 2000	23 Jan 2001	metal
2012	04 Feb 2012	22 Jan 2012	water

BUNYIP
THE AUSTRALIAN DRAGON

The bunyip, according to the stories of
Australian aborigines, is an evil spirit. It
dwells in creeks, swamps, and billabongs.
Early white settlers tell of encounters with the
bunyip. Most portray a creature with a hairy,
horselike head and a large body.

Modern sightings of the animal demand a
different explanation. One is that the
prehistoric diprotodon, thought to be
the largest marsupial ever to have
existed, is still around. There are
other explanations, but none of
them is more convincing than
the others.

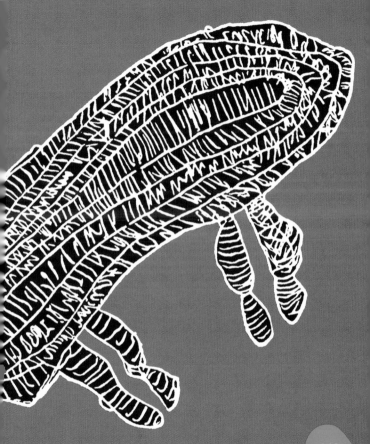

219

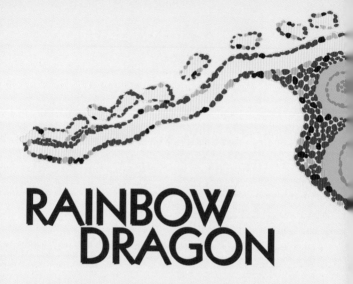

RAINBOW DRAGON

The significance of the rainbow serpent among
the aboriginal people of Australia is so great that
it has been called "the agent of destiny."
This being inhabits deep waterholes and is
known as a benevolent protector of its people as
well as the punisher of whoever breaks the law.

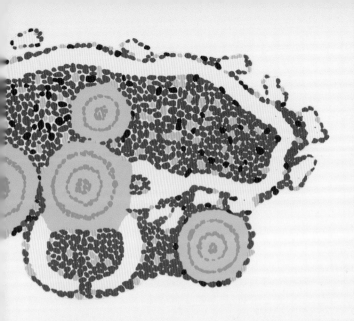

Representations of the rainbow serpent are to be
found in many forms and in many regions.
Many of them are believed not to be of human
origin, but "shades" of the serpent itself left in
the country during its travels.

TANIWHA

The taniwha is a monster believed by the Maori people to hide in the ocean and inland waters of New Zealand. Legend has it the Waikato River contains a hundred of them, one on each bend. The taniwha is usually depicted as an enormous tuatara-like beast, covered with traditional Maori Koru. The taniwha is often thought to be a cryptid—some kind of surviving prehistoric marine reptile.

A taniwha caused some controversy recently when a Maori tribe redirected the route of one of New Zealand's freeways to save the home of their legendary protector.

6

Real dragons

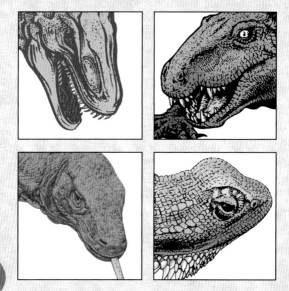

Real dragons have a lot in common with imaginary ones. In New Zealand, Australia, and Indonesia you can run into animals that appear to be creations of a wild imagination. Elsewhere, most real dragons are now only found in museums.

TUATARA

The tuatura is the sole relic of a group of reptiles that were widespread over 200 million years ago. It now only lives on islands off the coast of New Zealand. It has hardly changed in 140 million

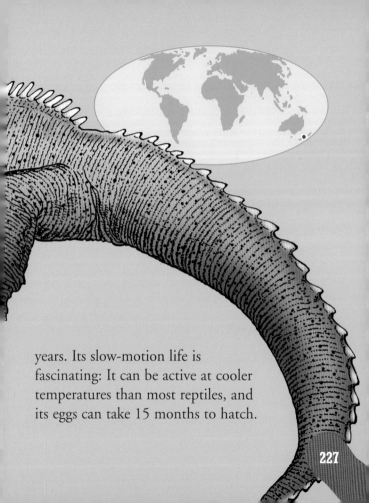

years. Its slow-motion life is fascinating: It can be active at cooler temperatures than most reptiles, and its eggs can take 15 months to hatch.

BOYD'S ANGLE-HEADED DRAGON

Boyd's angle-headed dragon (*Hypsilurus spinipes*) is also known as the Rainforest Dragon and is common in Australia. It is about 12 inches (30 cm) long, and weighs up to 2 ounces (60 g). It can change color according to its mood and environment.

229

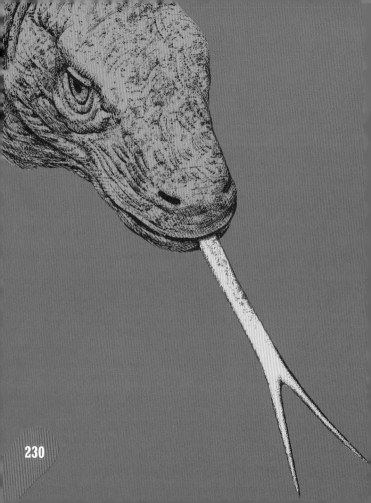

Komodo dragon

The Komodo dragon (*Varanus komodoensis*) is the largest lizard in the world. It can grow up to 10 feet (3 m) long and weighs around 150 pounds (70 kg).

They are carnivorous and mostly prefer carrion, but they can also hunt.

At least twelve human deaths have been attributed to Komodo dragon bites since records began in 1910.

Komodo dragons live on the Lesser Sunda Islands in Indonesia.

They are good swimmers. Perhaps that is how they spread between the islands. Seeing them in the water must have aroused fear in those who saw them.

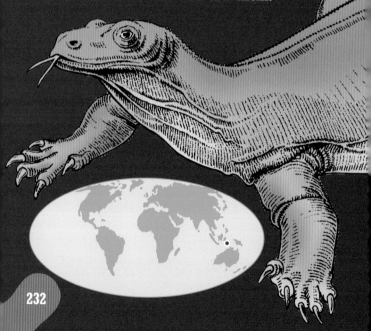

Komodo dragons also
conform to the mythological
association of fire and
dragons. They don't smell through
their nostrils—they use their
tongues, which flick in and
out like small flames.

233

ASIAN FLYING
DRAGONS

Flying dragons do not really fly—they jump from trees and glide. They live in the tropical forests of India and Southeast Asia, including Borneo and the Philippines. They never glide when it is raining or when it is windy. They have low, long bodies, and flaps of skin along the ribs that can be extended into "wings" when the lizard elongates its ribs. Flying dragons grow to slightly less than 12 inches (30 cm) in length.

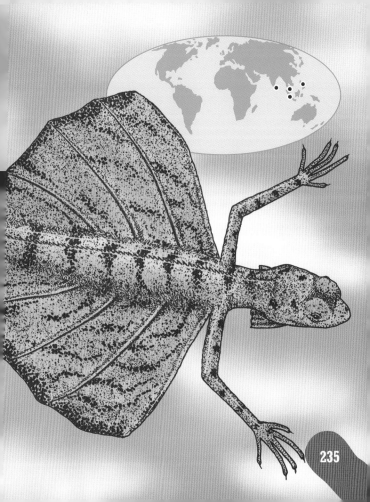

235

The frilled lizard

The frilled lizard or frilled dragon lives in Papua New Guinea and northern Australia. It has a ruff of skin that is usually folded back against its head and neck. When startled, the lizard opens its mouth wide and the frill flares outward, showing bright red and orange scales. Frilled lizards are gray, brown, or reddish-brown and grow up to 3 feet (1 m) in length. They walk on four legs, but can run on their hind legs when frightened. Because of this behavior they are known as "bicycle lizards" in Australia.

236

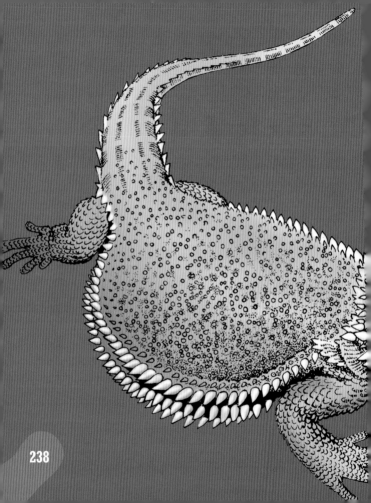

238

The bearded dragon

The Central or Inland Bearded Dragon is a type of agamid lizard found in the Australian desert. This dragon is the most commonly seen lizard in pet stores throughout the world.

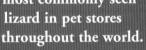

240

DRAGON FISH

Dragonfish combine camouflage with poison on their fins. With its spines spread, it looks like a dragon ready to charge.

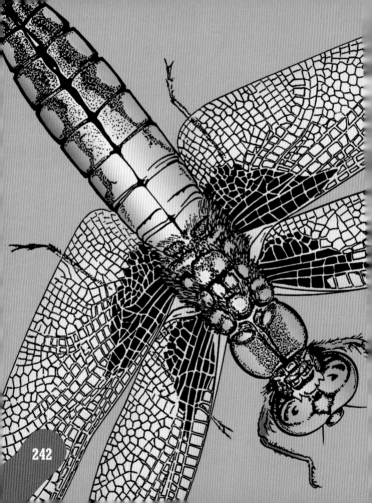

242

Dragonfly

The dragonfly could have been mistaken for a small dragon in the past: In Jurassic times, dragonflies were as big as seagulls. Nearly 150 million years before the first known birds flew, proto-dragonflies, the Meganeura, zoomed over hot swampy forests with wingspans as wide as a modern hawk's.

243

PUSHING IT TOO FAR

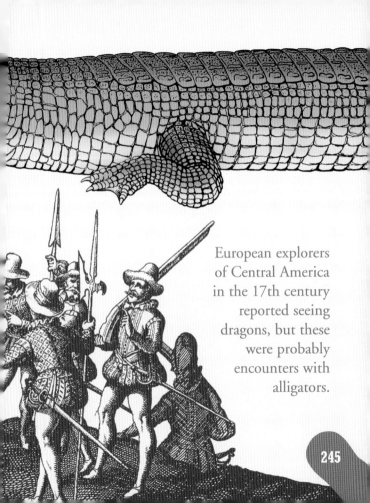

European explorers
of Central America
in the 17th century
reported seeing
dragons, but these
were probably
encounters with
alligators.

DRAGONS FROM THE DISTANT PAST

Dragon myths probably don't originate with the real giant lizards of prehistory, the dinosaurs, even though they obviously look similar.

Dinosaur means "terrible lizard." Fossils show they had scaly skin and tails, like modern reptiles. The first artistic reconstructions of these prehistoric dragons, in the 19th century, showed them as either two- or four-legged plant eaters. Some were enormous, but others grew little bigger than a chicken.

Dimetrodon, a carnivorous
mammal-like reptile

DIPLODOCUS

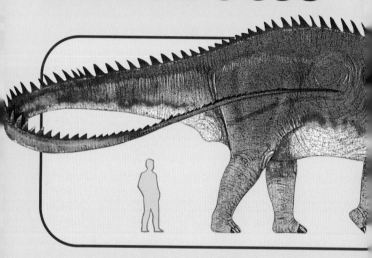

Like all dragons, *Diplodocus* had a long tail, and like some dragons, a long neck—but it was a real animal! This was the longest dinosaur that ever

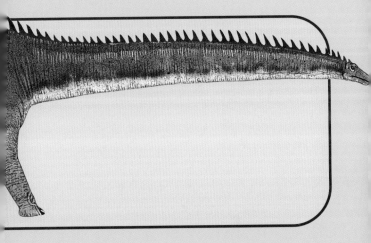

lived. It was longer than a tennis court. Just like all dragons, it had a spiny frill running down its back.

DRAGONS OF
THE SKY

Reconstructions of the bones of some prehistoric flying creatures resemble dragons. These discoveries of flying monsters came many centuries after the legends of dragons evolved.

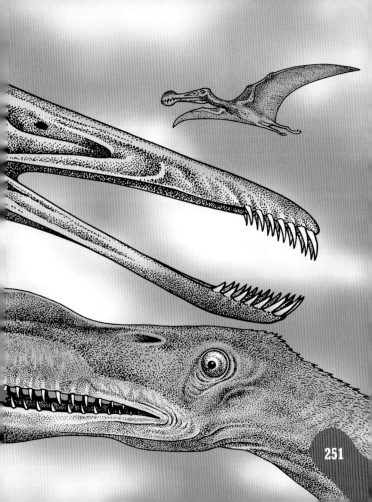

251

DRYPTOSAURUS

Dryptosaurus, or "wounding lizard," had short but powerful arms and great muscular legs. It was once believed that it used its huge hind limbs to leap on prey like a kangaroo, then kill with its eagle-clawed feet. Clawed feet and the ability to leap are some of the commonest dragon features.

MEGALOSAURUS

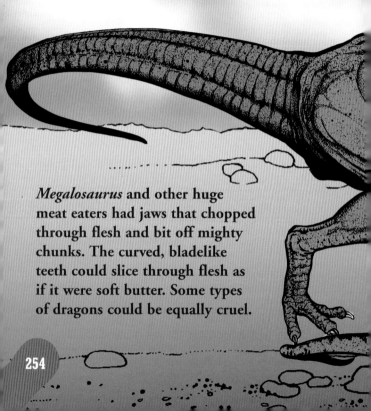

Megalosaurus and other huge meat eaters had jaws that chopped through flesh and bit off mighty chunks. The curved, bladelike teeth could slice through flesh as if it were soft butter. Some types of dragons could be equally cruel.

255

TYRANNOSAURUS

Tyrannosaurus probably preferred to take the easy option of eating dead flesh rather than biting living prey as some of its long teeth may have snapped off in a fight. Human imagination created dragons that share features with this prehistoric beast.

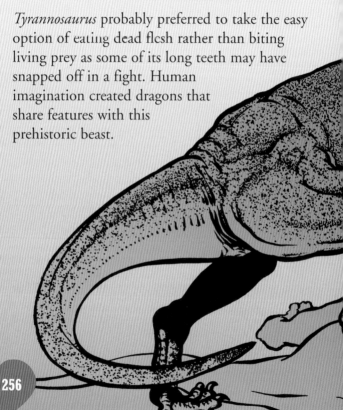

DEINONYCHUS

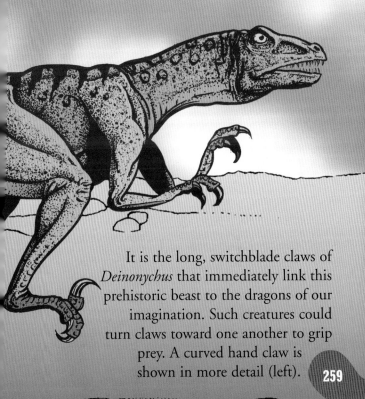

It is the long, switchblade claws of *Deinonychus* that immediately link this prehistoric beast to the dragons of our imagination. Such creatures could turn claws toward one another to grip prey. A curved hand claw is shown in more detail (left).

7
Dragon types

Mythological creatures have some of the features of dragons. Some of them have been given wings and others left to cope without them. Huge nostrils, sharp claws, and a sinuous tail have all played roles in the creation of mythological monsters.

HYDRA

The hydra is a serpentlike water beast of Greek mythology, with many heads and poisonous breath.

Hercules killed the hydra as one of his labors, but only with the help of his nephew Iolaus.

Each time Hercules severed one of the heads, two grew back. Eventually Iolaus suggested burning the stump each time a head was severed. This worked until only the immortal head was left, which Hercules then buried.

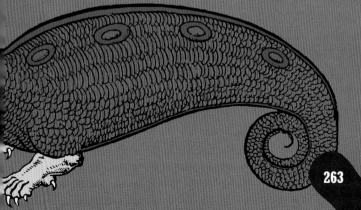

DRAKE

Serpentlike creatures called drakes have been part of European mythology for a long time.

Although a drake usually has wings it is generally found underground, hiding in its lair.

The dragons of European and Middle-Eastern mythology share their origins—a cult of snakes—with other world religions.

WYVERN

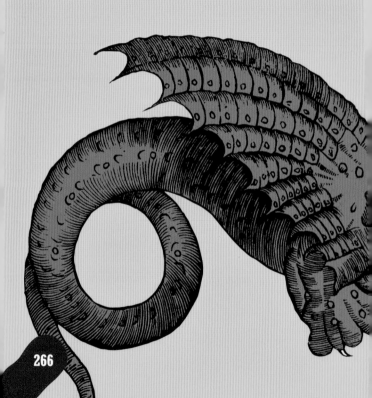

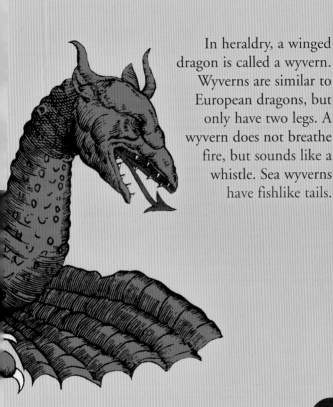

In heraldry, a winged dragon is called a wyvern. Wyverns are similar to European dragons, but only have two legs. A wyvern does not breathe fire, but sounds like a whistle. Sea wyverns have fishlike tails.

WORM

Worms are wingless, legless dragons that used to be very common in England. They usually lived in forests or wells, or close to any source of water.

Worms have always been linked to the Devil or demons. In the Middle Ages they sometimes had wings, but never legs. Destroying a worm meant killing the Devil himself.

The winged legless Lindwurm, a dragonlike serpent of Teutonic folklore

269

GRIFFIN

A griffin is a mythical beast with the body of a
lion and the head and wings of an eagle. It
sometimes has a serpentine tail.

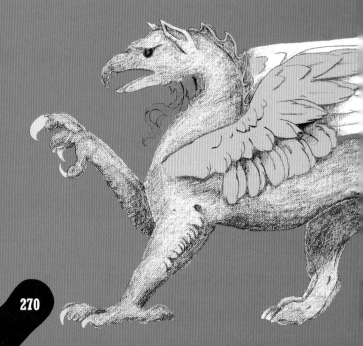

COCKATRICE OR BASILISK

A cockatrice, or basilisk, is a serpentlike creature that preys on crocodile eggs. It frequently appears in heraldry.

A basilisk attacked by a dog (left)

A basilisk in heraldic pose (right)

273

SPHINX

The Sphinx is a creature of Egyptian mythology that was also later used by the ancient Greeks. It is a winged lion with the head of a woman and tail of a serpent. According to the Greeks, Hera sent the Sphinx to sit outside Thebes and ask visitors the famous Riddle of the Sphinx:"Which creature walks on all fours

in the morning, on two at noon, then three in the evening?" Anyone unable to answer was strangled, but Oedipus solved the riddle—*Man*: as an infant he crawls on all fours; as an adult walks on two feet; finally in old age he needs a walking stick.

275

KRAKEN

The kraken is a huge sea monster similar to a gigantic lobster. They have been sighted off the coasts of Norway, Sweden, and Iceland. Marine monsters were commonly reported by Scandinavian seafarers in the 16th century, but the kraken's size made it particularly terrifying.

A kraken pulling a man overboard

A sea monster swallows a ship

ROC AND EAGLE

A roc, or rukh, is an enormous mythical white bird that can lift and eat elephants. There were sightings of this bird in the 16th century by English travelers in the Indian Ocean.

Just as the lion is the king of beasts, the eagle is the ruler of birds. It is a ferocious bird, symbolizing might and power.

A prehistoric bird, the Titanis, lived 2 million years ago. It resembled a roc, but couldn't fly.

The Arabic tale *Sinbad the Sailor* describes an encounter with a roc.

INDEX

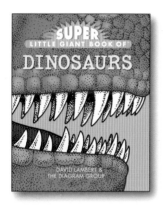

SUPER
LITTLE GIANT BOOK OF
DINOSAURS

DAVID LAMBERT &
THE DIAGRAM GROUP

SUPER
LITTLE GIANT BOOK OF
Prehistoric
Creatures

David Lambert &
The Diagram Group

SUPER
LITTLE GIANT BOOK OF
UNDERSEA
CREATURES

DAVID LAMBERT
& THE DIAGRAM GROUP

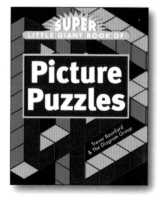

SUPER
LITTLE GIANT BOOK OF
Picture
Puzzles

Trevor Bounford
& The Diagram Group

SUPER
LITTLE GIANT BOOK OF
SECRET CODES
THE DIAGRAM GROUP

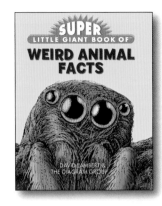

SUPER
LITTLE GIANT BOOK OF
WEIRD ANIMAL FACTS
DAVID LAMBERT &
THE DIAGRAM GROUP

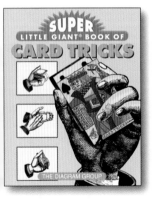

SUPER
LITTLE GIANT® BOOK OF
CARD TRICKS
THE DIAGRAM GROUP

SUPER
LITTLE GIANT® BOOK OF
MAGIC TRICKS
THE DIAGRAM GROUP